Little-Known Sports

To Dick,

On a good night at
Concordia.
        Best g luck,
        Vern Rutsala

Little-Known Sports

Vern Rutsala

University of
Massachusetts Press   *Amherst*

Copyright © 1994 by

Vern Rutsala

All rights reserved

Printed in the United States of America

LC 93-34630

ISBN 0-87023-917-1 (cloth); 918-X (pbk.)

Designed by Milenda Nan Ok Lee

Set in Walbaum

Printed and bound by Thomson-Shore

Library of Congress Cataloging-in-Publication Data

Rutsala, Vern.

Little-known sports / Vern Rutsala.

p.   cm.

ISBN 0–87023–917–1 (alk. paper).

ISBN 0–87023–918–X (pbk.: alk. paper)

I. Title.

PS3568.U83L57   1994

811'.54—dc20   93–34630

CIP

British Library Cataloguing in Publication data are available.

To Joan

For what do we live, but to make sport for our neighbors, and laugh at them in turn?

—Jane Austen

In La Mancha province, I possess seven and a half acres of quicksand on which I organize sinking contests. . . . The rules are simple. . . . The last to disappear wins.

—Pierre Bettencourt

What geneticists call a "sport"—a freak, a mutant. Doesn't fit any category.

—Richard Roud

Fertility
Today I feel fine, a real Balzac; I'm finishing this line.

—Augusto Monterroso

. . . the poem of life.
Of the pans above the stove, the pots on the table . . .

—Wallace Stevens

Don't worry about the horse being blind just load up the wagon.

—John Madden

Water won't boil on a cold stove.

—Cynthia Abbott

I'm no stranger to the temptation of the flesh. . . I confess that I give in almost daily (except Fridays when we have fish) . . .

—Gunter Eich

Contents

Little-Known Sports

Acknowledgments

Thanks are due the editors of the following periodicals in which the work printed here originally appeared:

The American Poetry Review: Tedium; Getting Lost; Hating; Being Hopeless; Deliberate Misunderstanding

Antenna: Smoking

Chicago Review: Orofino; Interruptions

The Greenfield Review: Getting into Bed; Hangover; Stupidity; Being with It

The Mississippi Review: Salt and Pepper; Dust Mop; Ironing Board; Tea Pots; Hesitation; Sleeping; Radio; Tables

Nebraska Review: Flipping the Sixpence; Answering the Telephone

New Letters (University of Missouri): Pictures of Herr Keuner

Pendragon: Attic; Crudity; Lying

Poetry NOW: In the Natural History Museum; On Time; Fog; Politics; Lecturers; Offering Consolation; A Snapshot; The Photographer; Public Appearances; Failure; Being Second-Rate; Frogs and Ponds

Portland Review: His Sabbatical

The Reaper: Madame Aupick; Vitalie Rimbaud; In Shadow

Seneca Review: Lesson from Long Valley

Zone: Fruit Bowl

Writing Poetry, Barbara Drake, Harcourt Brace and Jovanovich, reprinted "Sleeping" and "Salt and Pepper"

The Art of
Photography and
Other Sorrows

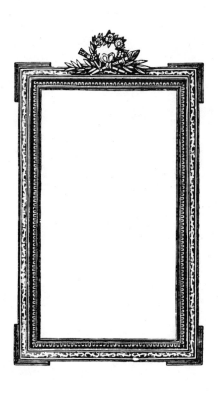

In Shadow

Off to one side, under the leaf shade, I spot myself staring toward the snapshot's deckled edge, curious apparently about something going on there, some marginal event, perhaps a stranger passing by or a dog on a dog's serious round. I've forgotten the lens and closed my ears to the photographer's directions and stepped back into the shade while the others, all strangers now, practice their various poses, each trying to win whatever prize it is that photographers always seem to offer. The strangers work hard at it, showing their teeth of different sizes and conditions, squinting quizzically, or raising their eyebrows with all the supercilious aplomb of eight-year-olds. So eager, so sure to win while I have done everything possible to take myself out of the picture without actually walking away. I still wonder what moves beyond the stiff margin, lying low behind the thick leaves that shade the house, watching.

The Photographer

You see him at every party, outfitted like a soldier with cases and tripods and those subtle lenses he likes to fuss over like a nanny. The shutter opens and closes so many times it seems to breathe and everyone readily falls into a pose when he nods. He likes this. He likes to nod and watch people vainly try to reveal their good sides, just as he likes to escape early with the evidence, the event rolled tight and secret in the camera's dry interior.

With the evidence in hand he loves the alchemy of dark-rooms —the liquids, the close darkness everyone must honor on pain of exposure. And he loves the mystery as pictures reveal themselves—fools' faces suspended in foolishness forever. And the marvellous thing: He is guiltless! He was no fool among fools. The others asked for this, they posed! They loved the music of the shutter and their own faces betrayed them into these grotesque images, their very skin his accomplice. He loves these moments and generously sends as many prints as you want.

Madame Aupick

This is her only known photograph. She is seated on the porch of the "Maison Joujou" at Honfleur. She wears black and seems to bar entrance to the house which rises around her with nearly perfect symmetry, a house like a well-structured book. Rising from what appears to be gravel or crushed seashells are seven steps, one for each sin, leading to the place where she sits. To enter the house you will have to ask her to rise and it has been too long—she will never rise. She will bar your entry forever, tiny as she is, dwarfed as she is by the "Maison Joujou"—which one suspects is merely a facade or, at best, one large cold room containing a single candle and a crucifix. Even through a magnifying glass Madame Aupick's face, in her only known picture, has no features at all.

Pictures of Herr Keuner

1922

Herr Keuner pretended to be reluctant to have his picture taken yet we have this, and other, early evidence. Dressed for a night on the town—suit, tie, jaunty cap—he looks tough and as if he is no longer poor B.B. out of the Black Forest. Clearly he's in town to stay and his politics are clear as well. In the three-quarters pose he looks to the left, his mouth set, his eyes clear though about both the mouth and the eyes there is the look of a suppressed smile, a smile he is trying to swallow, as he pretends to be a gangster.

c. 1935

Herr Keuner has found work and sits before his typewriter, large hands touching it with tenderness. The hair is short, he has for the moment at least abandoned his cap and suit—no longer on the town. Looking down at the page in the typewriter, he smiles rather sadly knowing how many more pages he will have to write and how each of them has already been sched-uled for a bonfire. It is now clear to him who the gangsters are.

1956

Showing his age and perhaps some hint of the death that will come later this year, Herr Keuner stares coolly at the camera with one eyebrow raised as if questioning the necessity of this interruption—there is still much work to do. He does, however, smile indulgently and poses his cigar for a portrait as well. Though he would scoff, the picture suggests very strongly that Herr Keuner has become a sage of the Eastern variety—without pomposity, willing to play the fool or even pose elf-like for his picture. He still knows who the gangsters are.

A Snapshot

She is caught in what can only be called an expansive gesture that is thrown out like a lasso to gather in everyone at the table.

The wine is motionless in its glasses, afraid even to ripple, every bubble has paused, listening, and you can all but hear her bracelets sliding together with their sound of counterfeit coins.

The lens even caught the glitter of a chandelier earring obeying the laws of physics as she tossed her head.

The fingernails—you must imagine this—make red arcs like landing lights, and, sadly, if you look long enough you begin to hear the famous laugh that shatters goblets and hopes.

Vitalie Rimbaud

She looks like no one so much as Alice with her large head, narrow shoulders, and child's body—and she is facing out from a corner as if she had just completed some punishment. But for her face there is no reason to believe that she is not Alice. The face is of an Alice who has come back through the looking glass and had some experience of this side's strangeness. The eyes and the mouth suggest this as do the severe eyebrows. Or perhaps she is simply preparing this face to meet what it must eventually meet. Examined more closely there appear to be things wrong with the room: The window is clearly opaque, perhaps merely drawn on the wall, and there seem to be smudged hex signs on the other wall—an angel being shot from a bow perhaps. Behind her the floor slopes downward, or appears to. The only truly reliable object is a chair which seems, however, to hang from Vitalie's wrist like a gigantic charm. Finally, we do not know which side of the mirror we are on or where poor Arthur may be.

Orofino

Orofino was the unspoken rumor, the waiting for letters, the bad news ready to happen. It was the place my father's stolen childhood lived, where denial waited to deny a final time. Everything not given would not be given once more. A whisper, a foggy postmark, a smuggled name faint as the circles of late night coffee cups as I ate my cereal. It was sachet and camphor, the feel of something hidden, something made of lace soaked in cologne. It was the dark bedroom beyond memory, the name Orofino. A meaning on a shelf just beyond my reach. An object the opposite of the hidden gift, some present that crumpled inward like a toadstool, ever inward and deep into wells deeper than our lake. The gift that was the absence of gift, the gift that took away, that ate, that demanded and denied. The gift that spent itself, that hollowed out, that drained light from the day. Orofino.

On Time

He is chewed steadily by his obsession with being on time. Thus his only event is arrival—after this there is nothing for him but the vacuity of interviews, jobs, all kinds of longueurs or entertainments during which he feverishly and covertly plans the intricate routes he must follow to meet his next appointment.

Lesson from Long Valley

You spend the whole day listening for footsteps, washed loose and drifting. And when it came you gave everything to fever, and now you can't find your shoes or your name. You listen. You question. What else can you do? Why did they make only your plow of tinfoil? Why did you get drunk and shoot the water bucket full of holes? All you remember is that Monday makes you thirsty, anything makes you thirsty. Your only conclusion is to pull out facts, hissing: And this! And this! And this!

Hesitation

*Hesitation of any kind is a sign of
mental decay in the young, of
physical weakness in the old.*
                    —Oscar Wilde

Greeted by choice we hesitate—a whole box of chocolates! A *dozen* eggs! Why not just one? We dream of that single egg, alone, perfect, asking only to be broken, promising nourishment and loyalty forever. Or there is the library—so many shelves, so many books! How can we choose the right one? Who will help us? We need a single thesis, not all these plurals, these theses. Confronted with riches we feel poor, knowing we will never choose, that we will always go away hungry, empty-handed, unlettered, and, finally, given all those roads to our houses, homeless.

Interruptions

We seem to live in a world populated only by men from Por-
lock. They keep lurching in shouting, "Excelsior!" Or is it, "Et
cetera!"? In any case they seem perpetually at the door so that
the only time we can't work is during that brief interval between their interruptions.

Fog

This is a new dimension. It makes outlines disappear and we become like faces on flowers or the animal shapes washed loose from rocks in river beds. Houses shift their sites in this mist. Addresses are shuffled. We walk among dead letters and wrong numbers. Slowly our skin grows scales and our fingers become webbed. We wince through this atmosphere, leery of the hot bite of hooks descending from someone's dream.

Politics

All day the tall king and queen, the knights and bishops, stare down imperiously at our hunched backs.

Lecturers

We have all seen those who are greatly admired and called 'dynamic' by people who like the sound of this word. The secret is that such lecturers exist solely to give meaning to that word, otherwise it would fall into disuse, and, to be truthful, the lecturers would then disappear like pierced balloons.

Offering Consolation

Our tongues are like mittens in our mouths.

Monsters

We are surrounded by monsters each day, but we have taught ourselves to move among them graciously, almost as if drugged, and never take note of their features. They do the same for us.

His Sabbatical

Routine has won and he wakes every day at the same time, then enters the dim brotherhood of drivers—each mounted behind glass. Still, he dreams between classes, writhing in the office where the radiator sweats and plots behind his back. He travels far, every inch of red tape snapped by his sprinter's chest. He strolls a ship's deck, talks of horseflesh with retired colonels in the bar. Ashore, he climbs mountains and follows unknown rivers to their source as easily as you move your finger in the phone book. He looks at sights and forgets them immediately and takes pictures with the lens cap on or throws the film away. He needs no record—this is life, he is there! Sometimes he finds a village where the Americano is loved by everyone and he writes a novel quickly, making no typographical errors. He hobnobs, his passport and his body stamped with royal seals, and goes from monastery to orgy freely as a milkman in the steaming tropics of that radiator.

Public Appearances

Actors and other public performers—especially politicians—are exaggerations. On stage or platform they seem perfectly natural, subdued or modest, self-effacing even, but when encountered in 'real life' they suddenly change. Their noses are too big, their voices too loud, their mouths like caves, and even their smallest gestures—such as striking a match—are like saber thrusts. What had appeared to be the delicately shaded art of the miniaturist turns out to be the rather careless craftsmanship of the barn painter.

Bestiary

Salt and Pepper

Monogamous as wolves they move through their lives together, rarely separated. To honor their feeling for fidelity we have developed the habit of asking for them together, knowing that they keenly feel any separation, however brief. Though salt is our favorite, a relative really, we never indicate this in order to spare pepper's volatile but delicate feelings.

Fruit Bowl

Actually, this is a shell whose creature has long since died. Long ago the ritual of its use was developed: Invert the shell and place in it, like prayers for a bountiful harvest, oranges, apples, bananas, whatever fruit was preferred. Now we only know that its fullness enriches our lives and its emptiness is always ominous, somehow entering us with the strength of a stern reproach. Though we are no longer believers we know we will never resort to the thoroughly secular practice of filling such bowls with wax fruit.

Dust Mop

This creature is some curious by-product in the evolution of the unicorn.

Ironing Board

It can fold its legs like a crane and is thus clearly some variety of bird no more grotesque than the pelican or the stork or, for that matter, the crane. It has three legs, for better balance, an enormous flat bill, and lives, as near as we can tell, on nothing but heat. A great solitary and apparently sexless—you rarely see more than one at a time—it is extremely docile and willingly nests anywhere you put it with its three legs drawn up tightly against its bill.

Tables

They are faithful as dogs and, like dogs, consider themselves central to the household. "Fundamental" is the word they use. Their hierarchy is intricate with, surprisingly, the dining room and kitchen tables looked upon as rather stolid beasts of burden —good fellows though rather stupid oxen finally. Coffee table has some status, comparable to that of lap dogs, though end tables rank rather higher, having as they usually do only one task—holding a lamp or an ashtray in place, for example—while the occasional table by virtue of its very name has dreams of possibility and is thus respected as a near member of the leisure class, but for utility and absence of labor coupled with an unending supply of gossip, the bedside table remains at the top of the list and nearly all the others aspire to his role.

Flowers

They are birds which spend their whole brief lives yearning for the sky, but they have planned their careers badly, going for bright plumage but no wings. A few do make it miraculously as far as the wallpaper where they become fossils, but most, finally recognizing their true condition, pluck out their feathers as quickly as they decently can, knowing the last one will say "loves me not."

Broom

Like the feather duster it feels incomplete, a creature only half evolved, and anxiously scurries everywhere trying to find the rest of itself.

Attic

Old creatures sleep here, so lazy they gather dust and seem scarcely to breathe. They appear this way because they are exhausted by their past lives and are content, lame and blind as some are, merely to graze in their peculiarly sedentary way. In fact, most consider their present status to be a reward for long and loyal service and would have it no other way, free as they are in their inertia of the chaotic lives downstairs.

Cobwebs

Over and over they try to spin the single thread that will lead us safely past the minotaur and finally free of this labyrinth. But they suffer from nerves—they drop a stitch, they panic, and in desperation refer it all to a committee, which produces this result.

Radio

This of course is the parrot that says whatever it wishes.

Telephone

Like the rattlesnake it has the decency to make a noise before it strikes though it is, of course, capable of imparting far more venom than any snake.

Desk Blotter

We thought we could teach this one to write but there is no known cure for his obsessive dyslexia.

Paperclip

We persist in baiting this dull hook with page after page, yet we catch nothing.

Tea Pots

There is about tea pots something of the domestic hen—that full rounded body and tail, a beak as well. And because they come and go fairly regularly, mysteriously breaking, there may even be some kind of pecking order among them. Generally, though, we have a favorite which we feed every day—sometimes pampering it with more than one feeding—with its rather austere diet of dry leaves and boiling water. Oddly it never complains, but the tea kettle on the other hand screams and whistles steadily, even crowing at times like a rooster.

Thermostat

Like an anemone it clings fast and remains sensitive to the slightest touch, even of air.

Pillows

Be grateful that we play possum all night.

In the Natural History Museum

Whole armies of birds sit tensely on lacquered branches ready to fly south at any moment, but winter never comes. In another area tooled leather alligators sun themselves and try to digest dinners of kapok. Near them the pottery relic of a giant turtle's back exhibits the tracings of a stylus which outline the basic tenets of vague and pagan religions. (His jaw is set firmly as a prime minister's in time of war.) And the whale, whose true skin is reputed to be no thicker than the film on boiled chocolate, lies on a painted wave, his great flukes silent as the rusted cannon in the park.

Little-Known Sports

Sleeping

Though winners are rarely declared this is an arduous contest similar, some feel, to boxing. This fact can be readily corroborated by simply looking at people who have just awakened. Look at their red and puffy eyes, the disheveled hair, the slow sore movements, and their generally dazed appearance. Occasionally, as well, there are those deep scars running across their cheeks. Clearly, if appearances don't lie, they have been engaged in some damaging and dangerous activity and furthermore have come out the losers. If it's not dangerous—and you still have doubts—why do we hear so often the phrase, *He died in his sleep?*

Crudity

Oddly enough timing is crucial to this activity in that a particularly crude or boorish act must, to be successful, be observed. In isolation it scores no points at all or, at best, may be interpreted as an act of vandalism. Further, the appropriate audience is necessary and such audiences are not gathered easily. Thus a whole congress of qualities is required if one's effort is to prove effective and receive a decent score, the most essential of which is, inevitably and obviously, finesse.

Flipping the Sixpence

Like many modern games this had its origin in the nineteenth century among the British aristocracy. When done properly it was necessary to dress well, carry a silver-topped cane, as well as a ready supply of coins in a waistcoat pocket. The next phase was to select a street which had a liberal supply of beggars and then to stroll down it in groups of two or three and then flip sixpence pieces into the beggars' proffered hats. What made this a contest was the distance and consistency with which an aristocrat could flip his coins. Anything beyond ten feet was generally lauded and there are reports of one Lord who was consistently accurate from fifteen feet. Variants, despised by the British as typically American bastardizations, include The Rockefeller Dime in which the giver has the audacity to *hand* dimes to people. Other despised variants include throwing coins into certain equatorial harbors where the locals dive for them, which, say the British, is ludicrous because it emphasizes the skill of the diver over that of the thrower. The preferred method remains the flip with thumb and index finger and the preferred target a beggar's hat—though a busker's instrument case is at times permissible. The older and more destitute in appearance the beggar the better, of course. Thus far it has remained an amateur sport.

Tedium

This clever invention of the playwright Anton Chekhov has burgeoned over the years until it is now, among amateurs, one of the major activities of the middle classes of the Western world. The more experienced dress in black and tell people at random that they are in mourning for their lives over and over, in order it seems to induce tedium in their listeners. The more earnest participants, however, twiddle their thumbs a great deal and sigh deeply as afternoon descends into evening. Dinner for them is always boring and entertainment an absolute affliction. When someone is told he has won the contest for the day, he yawns.

Answering the Telephone

This sport is akin to gymnastics, relying as it does on strength and grace. The form to be followed is relatively simple, assuming one has the strength and requisite character to stay in training. The exercise itself is initiated at random, i.e., when the phone rings—thus what in golf is called an "outside agency" is fundamental. The player must then be prepared for the ring at all times which is rather harrowing, especially when compared to the thoroughly orderly procedures of gymnastics. Nevertheless the random factor is the true test of the player's alertness. Following the ring the performer's movements may be freestyle as long as the phone is lifted accurately and deftly from the cradle and, with minimal motion, raised to the correct position—the end with the wire must be in the vicinity of the mouth. The exercise is completed when the athlete says, "Hello."

Getting Lost

This is an activity which has about it the subtlety of Zen and can only be managed by thoroughly experienced travellers or, at the very least, long-time residents of a particular neighborhood. The simple aim of course is to get lost and in doing so experience those emotions of doubt and strangeness, alienation, and, yes, even panic which, for the experienced player, is especially exhilarating. The trick then is to accomplish this deftly within familiar surroundings, areas that are literally known like the back of your hand. The venerated masters are those who are capable of getting lost a few doors from their houses. All aspire, however, to achieve the truly legendary feats of that revered grand master who is reputed to have gotten lost every day for a year though he never left his easy chair. Such genuine mastery is humbling indeed, but needless to say it is also inspiring.

Smoking

Like cock fighting or pit bull contests this is rapidly becoming an outlaw sport though many still engage in it rather openly and with a certain nervous bravado. There are some as well who practice it surreptitiously in forbidden rooms and elevators, taunting the law with disdain. Others practice it in private as single consenting adults.

Homage

There are various solitary sports such as thumb twiddling,
discreet scratching, looking at oneself in the mirror—all rather
vaguely narcissistic to be sure but relatively harmless, at least
to others, implying as they do only self-regard. The best of
them, however, was practiced by a doctor in New Jersey who
danced naked by himself late at night.

Hangover

The competition here is fierce and long, but few records have been kept just as few competitors ever truly witness another's score. This remains secret—a ballot no one marks—though there is a good deal of talk about it, like fishermen describing the one that got away. The true player simply endures whatever the previous night has given him. Cheaters, who are frowned on if the true player is capable of a frown, resort to a hair of the dog. True players hold such actions in contempt while they stare into the metaphysical distance and move with great care through the morning hours.

Failure

This, too, is Zen-like in its subtlety. The aim is simple: To lose. The trick though is that this must be accomplished in a way which doesn't acknowledge the possibility of defeat until it is a fact. There may be, for example, no suggestion of a fix, of taking a dive. The genuine failure approaches victory with confidence and aplomb and has it quite clearly within his grasp, but then, through a series of complicated maneuvers, he draws steadily away from winning until he arrives at his true goal—abject defeat which for him ensures his success.

Frogs and Ponds

A severe variant of snakes and ladders, this is generally practiced by the second-rate in any environment though it is per-
formed particularly well by those who have chosen to be big
frogs in small ponds. Usually such frogs designate their own
size, a peculiarity of this activity, by giving themselves titles
of various kinds—editor, dean, chairman, provost, chief, vice
president, and so on. Such titles, unfortunately, cannot influ-
ence biology. A small frog remains small whatever the size of
his pond.

Hating

The danger here is obsession and the truly adept avoid this with singular finesse. The obsessed are over-trained and nearly always drop out of the competition very early—like runners whose thigh muscles knot and cramp. The best performers select their objects of hatred with care and a degree of austerity, ignoring the scattergun approach which weeds out the inept. With one or two objects they are capable of carrying on normal lives while devoting a certain amount of disciplined attention to those objects. The objects, of course, are also crucial and the adept usually choose something quite simple—an ashtray or a calendar—while the bunglers choose large ungainly objects such as Nature or The Government. The adepts' hate is not a blinding or engulfing flame, rather it is like a firm and steady pilot light that never goes out.

Stupidity

The competition here is enormous—a daily Olympics in fact—though certain guidelines have been ineptly drawn up over the years. Still, the burgeoning numbers of contestants remain a genuine problem, but the guidelines which prevail, scrawled ungrammatically and illegibly, seem to indicate a means of classification which helps to limit the number of contestants. The main groups are, first, politicians, then administrators of all types, followed by generals and editors.

Getting into Bed

Some approach this with indifference, misunderstanding it as so many misunderstand the daily. Others, however, approach it with the care and attention to detail of mountain climbers. There is about their actions an air of ritual as they give this nightly activity its proper respect. Once they have prepared themselves physically and outfitted themselves with the proper equipment—bed, mattress, sheets, blankets, pillow and case, alarm clock, etc.—they approach the bed matter-of-factly.

For the act itself several techniques are available. There is, for instance the Fosbury Flop whereby the participant sits on the edge of the bed and rolls backward and to his right, aiming the back of his head at the pillow. Another method is the Western Roll—a swift knife-like leap under the covers. Some practice variations of the scissors stride, and there are also rather baroque freestylers who try to ring changes on the established methods. All approaches have their dangers and if not conducted properly the participant may spend a sleepless night, or, worse, may miss the bed entirely and suffer a painful injury. Though it is a less demanding game many prefer to play doubles which has its virtues.

Lying

In that you can have any number of opponents this can be a very difficult endeavor, requiring as it does an intricate, double-entry method of keeping score. The truly excellent, of course, juggle their score cards with ease, knowing as they do so that the real problem lies elsewhere: In order to lie successfully you quite simply must know what the truth is. As philosophers have persistently told us this is no easy task, and, because of this, there is some reason to believe that the truly outstanding liar lies out of a strong sense of modesty.

Being with It

Sunshine is a good example. Having come of age in 1968 as Betty Lou Balloon of Odessa, Texas, she immediately changed her name to Sunshine. Lately she has achieved one of her primary goals, allowing her as she says, to like actualize her potential: She is the proud possessor of a loom and a word processor. She now works fairly steadily on the former and needs the latter so that she may like share her health food recipes with her sisters. Thus far her only original recipe is one for macrame and cheese.

Being Second-Rate

There are people—and institutions—which quite clearly relish this activity. The pleasure is derived both from the warmth of many companions—as at the start of a marathon—and the avoidance of any pain which is—also as in a marathon—reserved for the leaders.

Being Hopeless

Requiring diligence and dedication this is something like killing all the flowers in your garden and encouraging the weeds—but that is only a metaphor. What must be done initially is to select a face—*woebegone* is the scientific term—and learn to wear it at all times. Choosing the right enemies will also help. Then you must systematically crush each hope as it appears, swiftly and efficiently, the way your grandmother used to wring the necks of chickens. If done with care you may become truly hopeless and therefore entitled to wear the most hangdog look at the most hilarious parties.

Deliberate Misunderstanding

Obtuseness is often confused with its counterpart, deliberate misunderstanding. It is an unfortunate confusion, mixing up as it does the clear definitions between the professional and the amateur, artist and hack. The obtuse performer, for whatever reason, simply does not comprehend, whereas the performer who deliberately misunderstands *knows* but pretends not to. The tragedy, of course, is that if the latter is found out he loses his professional standing, but if he is not found out he is simply branded obtuse.

This volume is the nineteenth recipient
of the Juniper Prize
presented annually by the
University of Massachusetts Press
for a volume of original poetry.
The prize is named in honor of
Robert Francis (1901–87),
who lived for many years at
Fort Juniper, Amherst, Massachusetts.